For Shawn and Adrienne

Library of Congress Catalog Card Number 92-32821
ISBN 0-7847-0040-0
Cataloging-in-Publication data available
Designed by Coleen Davis

The Standard Publishing Company, Cincinnati, Ohio
A division of Standex International Corporation
© 1993 by The Standard Publishing Company
Printed in the United States of America
00 99 98 97 96 95 94 93   5 4 3 2 1

I LIKE
Sunday School!

written by Mikal Keefer
illustrated by Joe Stites

LITTLE DEER
B·O·O·K·S
PSALM 42:1

Standard Publishing
Cincinnati, Ohio

I LIKE Sundays!
On Sunday morning, I go to Sunday school.

I get up early.

I help my mom and dad get up early, too.

On Sunday morning,
my whole family
eats breakfast together.

I wear my best clothes.
Dad helps me
shine my shoes
and knot my tie.

Now I have
my Bible,
so I'm ready to go.

I help Dad drive the car.

Mom and Dad take me
to my Sunday school class.
Then they go to a big-people class.
(They don't get snacks.)

My teacher, Mrs. Olmsted,
is glad to see me.
So are Nick and Jenna
and Shawna.

I used to be scared when Mom and Dad left me

But they always come back, so now I'm not afraid.

There are blocks and books at Sunday school.
But there aren't any toys that shoot or squawk
or use batteries.

I drop my quarter in the offering basket all by myself.

We sing about Jesus.
I sing very loud.
Mrs. Olmsted calls me her "joyful noisemaker."
When we pray, Nick asks God to bless his cousin.
Shawna asks God to heal her finger.
I ask God to save us from slimy,
wart-tongued monsters.
He always does.

We have Bible story time.
My favorite is about Noah and the ark.
I wish I had that many pets.

At snack time we have pretzels.
I ask for two.

During craft time we make arks
out of sticks from ice cream bars.
But we don't get the ice cream.

Mrs. Olmsted gives us our papers.
My dad likes to read the Bible story
to me at bedtime.